Planting a Rainbow

Written and illustrated by
Lois Ehlert

Harcourt, Inc.

SAN DIEGO   NEW YORK   LONDON

DEDICATED TO SHIRLEY AND DICK

Library of Congress Cataloging-in-Publication Data
Ehlert, Lois.
Planting a rainbow.
Summary: A mother and child plant a rainbow of
flowers in the family garden.
ISBN 0-15-262609-3
ISBN 0-15-262610-7 pb
ISBN 0-15-262611-5 oversize pb
[1. Gardening—Fiction. 2. Flowers—Fiction.
3. Mother and child—Fiction.]
I. Title.
PZ7.E3225P1   1988   [E]   87-8528

U T S R Q P O N M L

Printed in Singapore

Every year Mom and
I plant a rainbow.

In the fall we buy some bulbs

orange
tiger lily
bulb

TIGER LILY

red
tulip
bulb

TULIP

orange
tulip
bulb

TULIP

and plant them in the ground.

DAFFODIL

yellow
daffodil
bulb

blue
hyacinth
bulb

HYACINTH

purple
crocus
corm

CROCUS

purple
bearded iris
rhizome

IRIS

We order seeds from catalogs and

wait all winter long

Marigold

Cornflower

Aster

Daisy

for spring to warm the soil and sprout the bulbs.

TULIP

TULIP

DAFFODIL

HYACINTH

CROCUS

Then it's time to go to the garden center to select some seedlings.

We sow the seeds and set out the

plants in soil,

and watch the

TIGER LILY

DAISY

PHLOX

ASTER

CARNATION

ROSE

VIOLET

DELPHINIUM

rainbow grow,

and grow,

and grow.

tulips

carnations

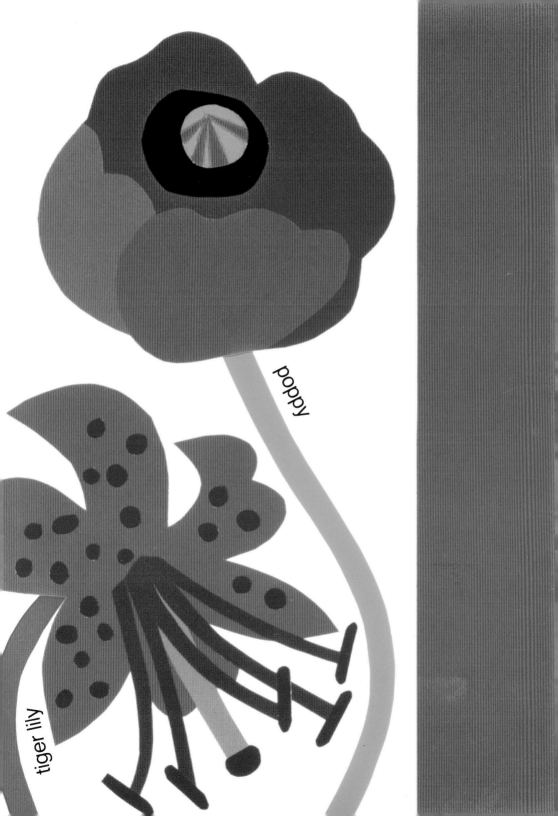

poppy

tiger lily

and some yellow blooms.

daisy

marigold

We have some red flowers

rose

zinnia

and
orange
flowers,

tulip

daffodils

We grow something green

ferns

and
some blue
flowers,

morning glories

delphinium

hyacinth

cornflowers

and some
purple
flowers,
too.

crocus

phlox

iris

violets

asters

pansy

All summer long
we pick them
and bring them home.

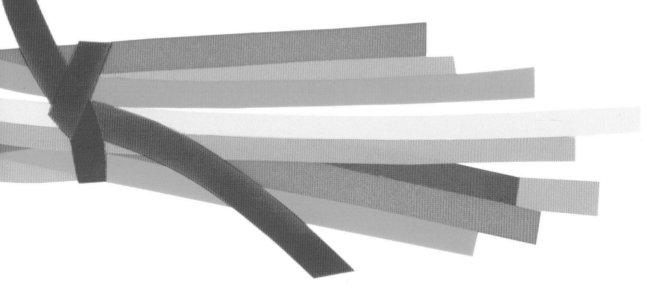

And when summer is over, we know we can grow our rainbow again next year.